# THE BEAUTIFUL GAME

# Alan Gibbons

# THE BEAUTIFUL GAME

With illustrations by
Chris Chalik

Barrington Stoke

*To all who fought so long and so hard
for justice for the Hillsborough families.
You'll never walk alone.*

First published in 2017 in Great Britain by
Barrington Stoke Ltd
18 Walker Street, Edinburgh, EH3 7LP

www.barringtonstoke.co.uk

Text © 2017 Alan Gibbons
Illustrations © 2017 Chris Chalik

The moral right of Alan Gibbons and Chris Chalik to be
identified as the author and illustrator of this work has
been asserted in accordance with the Copyright, Designs
and Patents Act, 1988

A CIP catalogue record for this book is available
from the British Library upon request

ISBN: 978-1-78112-691-2

Printed in China by Leo

# Contents

# Chapter 1
# The Big One

It was the big one.  Manchester United v Liverpool at Old Trafford.  Lennie was on his way there with Dad and Grandad – part of a crowd of singing, cheering Liverpool fans.  Lennie should have been confident.  The Reds were 2–0 up from the first leg.  Only he wasn't.  He was so tense he was almost shaking.

"Nervous?" Dad said.

"A bit," Lennie admitted.

Dad burst out laughing. Grandad slapped Lennie on the back and gave him a playful shove.

"A bit?" Grandad said. "Look at him! The boy can hardly breathe."

Lennie grinned. They were only teasing, but it was true. He was really stressed. It was bad when they lost, but to lose to Man U was the worst.

"We ripped them to bits at Anfield, didn't we?" Lennie said, to remind himself.

"Yeah, the Reds played them off the park," Dad agreed. "All we need is a draw tonight and we're into the next round. This could be our year."

Lennie nodded. In his head he replayed Daniel Sturridge's penalty and Roberto Firmino's goal late in the game. The memory made him smile.

"We're not going to give two goals away, are we?" he said.

Dad turned and patted his back. "No chance, son."

They walked across the big open space in front of United's stadium.

"The Theatre of Dreams," Dad said.

Grandad snorted. "Tonight, we'll give them nightmares."

Then Grandad pointed out the statue of Bobby Charlton, Denis Law and George Best.

"United's Holy Trinity," he told Lennie. "Their team today isn't a patch on the one they had back in the 1960s."

"Ancient history, Grandad," Lennie said with a grin, but he still asked, "Did you see them play at Anfield?"

Grandad shook his head. "I didn't go when I was your age."

"How come you didn't go?" Lennie asked. It seemed strange – Grandad was football crazy.

Grandad shrugged. "It's a long story. I'll tell you some other time."

They squashed through the turnstiles with all the thousands of other fans and made their way to their seats. The ground was nearly full, over 70,000 people. Lennie's tummy turned over. They couldn't lose. They just couldn't.

The whistle blew and then Lingard nearly scored for Man U with a header inside the box.

Lennie looked over at his dad.

"That was a bit too close," Dad said.

"Nice clean save by Mignolet," Grandad said.

There were chances for both sides then Nathaniel Clyne brought down Anthony 'Golden Boy' Martial in the area.

Lennie had his hands over his mouth.

"Oh no, we've let them back in it," he groaned.

"Steady," Grandad told him. "They haven't scored it yet."

But Martial made no mistake with the penalty.

United 1 Liverpool 0.

2–1 to Liverpool on aggregate.

Dad's face had turned serious.

"Game on," he said, and he clapped his hands. "Come on you Reds."

Now United were back in the tie, Old Trafford was bouncing with noise and energy.

"If they get another, we're in dead trouble," Lennie said.

This time, neither Dad nor Grandad said anything. They were feeling the pressure just as much as Lennie. There were grim faces all around. Not long after, Sturridge hit the bar. The Liverpool fans were all up out of their seats.

So close.

Just before half time, Coutinho picked up the ball and cut in from the left.

"Go on," Lennie said.

He went past his man.

"Go on, *go on*," Lennie urged.

Coutinho kept pressing forward, then he squeezed the ball past United's keeper, David de Gea.  The net bulged.  Lennie's heart pounded with joy.

*"Goal!"*

Now the three of them were punching the air and dancing.  Lennie couldn't stop laughing – Grandad could move for an old guy!

3–1 to Liverpool on aggregate.

After that, it wasn't long before the half time whistle blew.  The faces of the United fans were like stone.  Their team was on its way out of Europe.

"United have got too much to do," Dad said. "I think we've won it."

But Grandad said, "We need one more goal to be sure."

Lennie listened to them then something caught his eye.

"Look," he said, eyes gleaming. "Flares!"

Red smoke was rising into the evening sky.

Red for Liverpool, not United.

United huffed and puffed in the second half. They got more and more desperate, but Liverpool held tight and did their job. They defended well. It was still 1–1.

"It's in the bag," Dad said.

That's when Grandad pointed. "What's going on over there?" he asked.

Lennie turned to see a big group of stewards running over to a section of fans.

"Fighting," Dad said. "Idiots."

Lennie watched the crowd moving like a stormy sea. He could sense something wild and ugly in the air.

Some of the United fans were chanting at the Liverpool fans. They were singing one of Liverpool's songs back at them, but they had changed the words. Instead of *Liverpool, Liverpool, Liverpool*, it was *Murderers, Murderers, Murderers*.

Lennie flinched. Then he heard the word Hillsborough.

Lennie knew all about Hillsborough. Every Liverpool fan did.

96 Liverpool supporters – men, women and children – died at the FA Cup semi-final at Hillsborough in 1989.

Lennie heard the chants and his eyes stung. Liverpool fans had died and now the United supporters were calling them *murderers*! He stared at his dad as his stress about the match turned into something much worse.

"Ignore the trouble," Dad told him. "Focus on the game."

But the United fans weren't finished. They were chanting again, a sea of arms raised in accusation.

"*The Sun* was right," they called. "You're murderers."

*The Sun.*

That was the newspaper that had lied about the Liverpool fans and what had happened at Hillsborough. Lennie's fists were balled with anger, his heart thumping.

Just then, behind him, some of the Liverpool fans started to sing their own song –

"*Who's that dying on the runway?*"

Lennie had heard the song before. He was so upset, he joined in –

*"Who's that dying in the snow?*
*It's Matt Busby and his boys ..."*

Lennie didn't get to finish. His dad had grabbed his arm, hard. Why? Lennie was only giving as good as he got.

"They started it," he said.

Dad's face was grim.

"Watch the game," he said. "And no more of that rubbish."

Lennie frowned. "But ..."

"Don't say another word, Len," Grandad warned with a shake of his head. "Your dad's right. Watch the game and ignore those idiots."

There were no more goals.  When the final whistle went, Lennie celebrated, but he knew he was going to get told off.  Those chants had changed the mood at the game.

# WHAT HAPPENED AT HILLSBOROUGH?

On Saturday 15th April 1989 Liverpool played Nottingham Forest in the FA Cup semi-final at Sheffield Wednesday's Hillsborough stadium.  It became the worst sporting disaster in British history.

96 people died and 766 were injured.

English football had had big problems with hooliganism in the past so there were tall metal fences to stop fans getting on the pitch.

The fans who died were in the Leppings Lane end of the ground.  Eight years earlier, in 1981, 38 Spurs fans had been injured at the Leppings Lane end of the ground.  Then there were 10,100 fans in the Leppings Lane end – the police said that was far too many.  But, on the day of the 1989 disaster, there were far too many fans again.

When the police decided to open two extra gates because of the numbers coming into the ground, people were crushed to death.  Many police still thought their job was to stop fans getting on the pitch – not to keep them safe.

Some fans climbed over the fence to get away from the crush. All this time, the match was going on – but after six minutes the referee stopped the match. He knew something was very wrong.

Liverpool fans did their best to help the injured. They carried them on hoardings that they tore down.

At last, 44 ambulances arrived, but only one got into the ground. People died who could have been saved.

After the disaster, South Yorkshire Police blamed the Liverpool fans. The police said the crush happened because the fans were late for kick-off or they were drunk.

Then, on Wednesday 19th April 1989, *The Sun* published a front-page headline – 'The Truth'.

It repeated the lie that the Liverpool fans were to blame.

It said fans stole from the dying and peed on the police.

It said fans beat up police who were giving people the kiss of life.

None of it was true.

It took 27 years before the truth of what happened at Hillsborough was made public. All that time, the families of the dead fought for justice.

# Chapter 2
# The Worst Day of My Life

Lennie knew he was in trouble.

"What did I do wrong?" he asked.

"Let's get back to the car," Dad said. "This isn't the time or place."

Grandad agreed. "We can talk as we drive home," he said.

Nobody said very much as they followed the rest of the crowd out. Lennie was happy about the score, but he found it hard to understand why Dad was so angry with him. There was a lot of traffic as they left Old Trafford, but at last they got on the motorway.

"OK," Dad said. "Let's talk."

"Why did you stick up for the Mancs?" Lennie asked, straight off.

Lennie had been stewing about that. It wasn't fair. Why was he the one to get shouted at?

"Don't call them that," Dad told him. "Say 'United fans'."

"But why did you stick up for them?" Lennie asked again. "The *United fans*. They were chanting about Hillsborough."

"Yes," Dad said, "and some Liverpool fans were chanting about the Munich disaster. I don't think that helped much, do you?"

Munich.

Lennie knew it was an air crash, but not much else.

"The Mancs … I mean the United fans started it," Lennie said. "Our song was just a way of getting back at them."

Grandad tutted. "Sometimes you have to let things go, Len," he said. "Two wrongs don't make a right."

"You were at Hillsborough, Grandad," Lennie said. "So were you, Dad. Why aren't you angry?"

Dad took a deep breath but he kept his eyes on the motorway.

"I think about it every day," he said. "Hillsborough should have been one of the best days of my life. I'd never been to a big away game before. I was daft with excitement."

Dad went on, as they drove towards Liverpool.  "It was a nice day," he said.  "There was sun on the hills as we came into Sheffield.  It's a lovely drive over the Woodhead Pass.  Your grandad parked and we set off for Hillsborough.  It was a long walk."

"That's right," Grandad said.  "We parked a mile or two from the ground.  We had a bag of chips on the way."

"So what happened?" Lennie asked.

Dad took up the story again.  "By the time we got near to Leppings Lane, the place was packed, rammed.  It was really slow getting through the turnstiles.  There weren't enough of them.  We were nearly running.  There was a bit of a slope on the way into the ground."

Lennie put his arms on the back of the seat and leaned forward.

"When did you know something was wrong?" he asked.

"I didn't," Dad said. "It was crowded, but it was my first away match. I didn't know what to expect. The singing was a roar in my ears and there was this beach ball bouncing around the crowd."

"I knew something wasn't right," Grandad said. "It was hard to keep hold of your dad's hand. I was getting worried, but there were so many people behind me, I couldn't move."

"There's only one way I can describe it," Dad said. "It was like being in the sea when there are really big waves. I got lifted off my feet. I started to panic. Your grandad pulled me out."

Lennie turned to look out the window as an Aston Martin roared past.

"I did my best," Grandad said, "but I could hardly stay on my feet myself. It was hard to breathe. There were still twenty minutes to go until kick-off and the pressure was getting worse."

"I've never felt anything like it," Dad said. "I could feel a man's breath on the back of my neck. It was hot. I got a look at him and his eyes were popping. It was horrible. I couldn't move my arms at all. All the feeling was going out of my body."

Grandad nodded and looked across at Dad.

"I always thought I was strong," he said, "but I couldn't do a thing. It was that bad. I was sweating. My lungs were bursting. I was holding onto your dad for dear life. I thought I was going to lose him."

He shook his head and twisted his fingers in his lap.

"You could hear people yelling," he said. *"Open the gate! People are dying in here.* Some

of the coppers still didn't get it. They were telling us to calm down and move away from the fence."

"Fat chance of that," Dad said. "We were pushed right up against it."

Lennie tried to imagine what it must have been like.

"How did you get out?" he asked.

"To this day, I don't know," Grandad said. "I had to fight to get your dad away from the crush."

Lennie had never seen his grandad so upset. He was wiping the tears off his cheeks.

"I had to save my son," Grandad said. He took a deep breath. "In the end – somehow – we got onto the pitch. I hugged your dad to me, so glad we were safe. But then when I looked around there were people lying on the grass, dead and hurt so bad.  I've never seen anything like it."

No one spoke and a mile or two of motorway sped past.

Lennie broke the silence.  "Then *The Sun* said it was our fault."

Dad nodded.  "Yes, that was a proper kick in the teeth."

"People in Liverpool stopped buying *The Sun* after that," Grandad added.

They turned off the motorway and drove down Edge Lane towards home.

Lennie understood now.  "So," he said, "the United fans shouldn't have sung about Hillsborough."

"Of course they shouldn't," Dad said, "but it's just as wrong to sing about Munich."

Lennie turned to Grandad. "What happened at Munich?" he asked.

Grandad frowned. "I don't know why you're looking at me, lad. I was only a baby!"

"But you know what happened, don't you?"

The smile left Grandad's face as he thought about it.

"Yes," he said. "The United team were coming home from a European game in Germany. They were called the Busby Babes, one of the greatest sides ever. Then their plane crashed on the runway."

"And they all died?" Lennie said.

"They didn't all die," Dad told him. "Remember that statue of Bobby Charlton?"

"Yes."

"He was there."

"But he's really old!" Lennie said.

"He was a young lad back then," Grandad said, and he rubbed his bald patch. "We were all young once."

That made them laugh – and it was good to laugh after what Lennie had just heard.

"So no more singing about Munich, OK?" Dad said. "The Manchester lads are just like us. We've both had our bad times."

# WHAT HAPPENED AT MUNICH?

The Munich air disaster happened on Thursday 6th February 1958.

The Manchester United team of the time was one of its best ever. Everyone loved them. They were called the Busby Babes, after their manager Sir Matt Busby.

The team had drawn 3–3 against Red Star Belgrade to win a place in the semi-finals of the European Cup – the tournament that later became the Champions' League.

On their way home, the team's plane stopped at Munich to refuel. It was snowy and the runway was covered with slush. The pilot tried three times to take off – and, on the third attempt, the plane crashed.

23 people died. Among them were eight United players. One, Duncan Edwards, was one of the greatest English footballers of all time.

After the tragedy, Sir Matt Busby went on to build another great team, which won the European Cup ten years later.

There have been two other terrible air disasters involving football teams.

## 1949 – Turin, Italy

On 4th May 1949, 31 people died when a plane carrying the Turin football team – known as the *Grande Turino* – crashed into a wall at the back of the Basilica of Superga.  In memory of the victims of the crash, the wall has never been restored.

## 2016 – Colombia

On 28th November 2016, 71 people died when a plane carrying Brazil's Chapecoense team crashed in Colombia.  The Chapecoense players had risen from playing non-league football to contend for one of the biggest trophies in South America.  They were on their way to a Copa Sudamerica finals match against Atlético Nacional when 19 of the 22-man squad died in the crash.

# Chapter 3
# Fire and Disaster

The next day, Lennie was helping his little sister Layla with her reading homework. She didn't really need help – she was a good reader. The book was about New York, and Mojo the dog was looking at it over her shoulder, as if he was helping too. Then the doorbell went and Layla dropped her book and scrambled to the front door while Mojo bounced along beside her.

It was Gran and Grandad, round for Sunday dinner.

Layla led Gran inside, then jumped onto her knee to show her the New York book. It had a picture of super-tall skyscrapers and an old-fashioned fire engine on the front.

Lennie turned to Grandad.

"Why don't you work as a fire-fighter like my dad any more?" he asked. He was proud that his dad and grandad were fire-fighters, but all of a sudden he realised he had never asked why Grandad had stopped.

Gran gave Grandad a quick look, the kind that told him not to say too much. Lennie frowned. What was that about?

"There's nothing to hide," Grandad said, when he saw Lennie's frown. "Your gran doesn't want me to scare you."

"I don't get scared," Lennie said.

"Listen to Mr Tough Guy," Dad said as he walked in.

"Well, I don't," Lennie said.

Mojo wagged his tail and licked Lennie's hand.  At least he thought Lennie was very brave.

"Maybe not, but you worry," Dad said. "Remember that big fire last year?  You couldn't sleep till I got home."

"That's because your job's dangerous," Lennie said.  He turned to Grandad.  "So why don't you do it any more?"

"OK.  It's like this," Grandad said.  "We went into this blazing factory one time.  The place was full of chemicals and it could have exploded just like that."  He clicked his fingers, fast.  "Anyway, the floor gave way under me and I broke my leg and hurt my back.  The leg mended, but I've had trouble with my back ever since.  And I'm not far off retirement!  That's why I do a desk job now."

Lennie was worried.  He looked at Dad.  "Has anything like that ever happened to you?"

"There have been a few bad moments," Dad said with a shrug, "but I'm still standing, aren't I?"

"It was a bad fire, wasn't it?" Lennie asked. He could tell Dad was hiding something.

Dad still didn't want to talk.  So Grandad came to his rescue.

"I'll tell you when there was a bad fire," he said.  "It was a terrible thing.  Bradford City. 1985."

"Were you there?" Lennie asked.  He was interested – he'd never heard about the Bradford fire before.

"No," Grandad said.  "Me and your dad have done all our fire-fighting here in Liverpool."

"Was anybody hurt?" Lennie asked.

Grandad nodded.  "Not just hurt," he said. "There were more than fifty dead and over 200 injured."

Lennie stared in horror.  What a terrible way to die.  He couldn't believe that many people could be killed in a fire.

"It was another disaster waiting to happen," Grandad said.  "The club had been warned about the safety of the ground.  There was rubbish piled up under the main stand.  All it needed was a match or a cigarette end and the whole thing would go up like a tinderbox."

"And that's what happened?" Lennie asked.

"That's what happened."

Lennie thought about Hillsborough and about Bradford.  All those people – fans at football matches – dead and not so long ago.

"Why does this stuff keep happening?" he asked.

"I don't know," Grandad said.

"Yes you do," Dad said. His eyes were aflame. "Football started as the working class game. There were huge crowds in the old days, even bigger than today's, and most of the fans stood on the terraces. The clubs packed them in, and they never paid enough attention to safety."

"True," Grandad said. "Football has had its fair share of trouble. Ibrox, Burnden Park, Bradford, Hillsborough. The stadiums couldn't cope with the numbers."

Lennie didn't understand. "Why didn't they build better stadiums?" he asked.

Grandad tapped his nose. "They did in the end, but that costs money. They only improved the grounds after Hillsborough. That's when they took the fences down and brought in seating-only stadiums."

"They put the prices up too," Dad grumbled. "It costs a fortune these days.  It's always the fans who lose out."

That's when Gran butted in.

"Are you going to chat about football all afternoon?" she scolded as she shut Layla's book. "Your dinners are getting cold."

But dinner didn't stop Lennie thinking about football.

"I don't get it," he said, as he put his fork down.  "Football is about the fans.  They should treat them better."

"I agree," Grandad said.  "You should have seen the grounds in the old days.  The toilets were a disgrace."

Dad threw Mojo a piece of chicken and the little dog gobbled it up.

"Some of the fans didn't help," he said. "In the 1970s and 1980s there was a lot of fighting and hooliganism. Mind you," he said as he tossed Mojo another piece of chicken. "The clubs went over the top. They put the fans in cages."

"Cages?" Lennie said. "Like zoo animals?"

"Exactly like that," Dad said. "That's why Hillsborough was so bad. Nobody could get out. They were trapped. The clubs were more worried about stopping hooligans than keeping the rest of the fans safe."

Lennie had an awful thought.

"Were the fans in cages when the Bradford fire happened?"

"No," Dad said. "Thank God. Anyway, Lennie, you remember all this before you do any more shouting at Man U fans. We are all in it together."

Gran wagged her fork at Lennie. "I don't want you yelling at anybody. Do you hear? Your dad told me what you did."

"Sorry," Lennie said.

Mojo looked sad for Lennie. He didn't like it when anyone got told off.

"I won't do it again," Lennie said. He grinned. "Not even to Mancs."

Dad burst out laughing and looked at Grandad.

"Shall I tell him, Dad?"

"Tell me what?" Lennie asked.

"I'm going to introduce you to a friend of mine next week." Dad winked. "He's a big United fan."

Lennie's eyes went wide.  "Manchester United?"

"That's right," Dad said.  He rubbed Lennie's head as he got up to clear the table.

Lennie couldn't believe it.

"But you're a Scouser!" he said.  "How can you have a friend who's a Manc?  Scousers and Mancs don't mix!"

"You'll get it when you meet him," Dad said, with a laugh.

"Do I have to go?" Lennie asked.

"Yes," Dad said.  "You have to."

Mojo put his chin on Lennie's knee.

Manchester?

He didn't like the sound of that.

# THE HISTORY OF FOOTBALL DISASTERS

### 1923 – Wembley, London

Every football fan has heard of the 'White Horse' FA Cup Final, but few know that it could have been a major football disaster.

The Final was between Bolton Wanderers and West Ham United at Wembley. It was the first football match to take place at Wembley. The ground was meant to hold 125,000, but between 200,000 and 300,000 turned up.

Fans were everywhere – including on the pitch. Black and white news footage shows a policeman on a horse called Billie clearing space for the game. Billie was grey in real life – but looked white on the old film.

Disaster was averted. About 900 fans were hurt, but only 22 fans and two policemen had to go to hospital.

## 1902 – Ibrox Park, Glasgow

The first football disaster resulting in death was on the 5th of April 1902 when the West Stand at Ibrox collapsed. 25 fans were killed and 517 injured during an international between England and Scotland.

## 1946 – Burnden Park, Bolton

Over 85,000 people crowded into Burnden Park to watch a cup tie between Bolton Wanderers and Stoke City. Two walls collapsed. 33 people died and 500 were injured.

## 1971 – Ibrox Park, Glasgow

On Saturday 2nd January 1971, 66 people – among them many children – died in a crowd crush at the end of an 'Old Firm' match between Celtic and Rangers.

## 1985 – Valley Parade, Bradford

On Saturday 11th May 1985, a small fire that started in rubbish below an old wooden stand became the worst fire disaster in the history of football. 56 fans died and at least 265 were injured.  As a result of the tragedy, Bradford City F.C. continues to support the Burns Unit at Bradford Royal Infirmary.

## 1985 – Heysel, Brussels, Belgium

On 29th of May 1985, 39 fans died after fighting broke out between Liverpool and Juventus before the European Cup final.  Most of the dead were Italian.  A concrete wall collapsed, making things worse.  More than 600 people were injured.  Shockingly, the game still took place.  The disaster was described as "the darkest hour in the history of UEFA competitions".

## 1989 – Hillsborough, Sheffield

On 15th April 1989, 96 people died at Hillsborough. They were either crushed or suffocated in a terrible 'human crush'.  It remains one of the world's worst ever football disasters.  In September 2016, the 96 victims of Hillsborough were awarded the Freedom of the City of Liverpool, the first time the city has awarded its highest civic honour to people who have died.

# Chapter 4
# The Beautiful Game

Dad was cooking the tea when Lennie got home from school the next day.

"You're not serious, are you?" Lennie said.

"Serious about what?" Dad asked.

Lennie put his school bag down on the kitchen table as Mojo jumped up at him. "You know, going to Manchester."

"You didn't grumble last time," Dad said.

"We were going to a match," Lennie said. "The Europa League."

"We're going to a match this time," Dad told him. "We're going for a kick-around at Heaton Park. My mate's kids are good footballers."

Lennie still wasn't impressed. Then he thought of something.

"You know when we were at Old Trafford?" he said.

Dad nodded.

"Grandad said something funny."

"He does that."

"No," Lennie said. "I don't mean a joke. He said he didn't go to Anfield when he was young. Why not? He's the biggest Liverpool fan I know."

Dad's face turned serious. "Your grandad grew up in the 1960s, Lennie. Things were different back then."

"Different how?" Lennie asked.

"Well," Dad said, "most people outside Liverpool didn't even know there were black Scousers. We lived our lives in Liverpool 8. You didn't see many black people in the city centre, not in shops or pubs or on the street."

"How come?" Lennie asked.

"Liverpool was a lot more racist then. Everywhere was. It was the same with the football clubs. Liverpool and Everton were all-white teams."

Lennie thought of all the black players at the city's two clubs now. It was hard to believe it hadn't always been this way.

"Grandad could still have gone to the matches," Lennie said.

"It wasn't that easy," Dad said. "Black kids who went out of the area got chased or beaten up by gangs. People would spit at you in the street, call you names. It happened to me a few times."

Lennie stared at his dad. "That's disgusting."

"Of course it is," Dad said. "That's the way things were back then." He looked at Lennie. "Has it ever happened to you, son?"

Lennie thought. "I've had a bit of name-calling." He turned away. "I had one fight."

"Why didn't you say anything?" Dad asked.

"You're always telling me not to fight," Lennie said.

Dad laughed and put his arms round Lennie. "You've got me there, son."

Then he put the lid on the pan, sat down at the table and flipped open the laptop.

"Let's play a game," he said to Lennie, and he patted the seat for him to sit next to him.

"Name Liverpool's first black player," Dad said.

"Easy," Lennie said. "John Barnes."

"Wrong," Dad said. "Here he is."

Lennie looked at the guy on the screen. "Who's that?"

Dad grinned. "Meet Howard Gayle. He was a winger. Strong and super fast. He was from Liverpool 8."

"Liverpool 8!" Lennie said.

"That's right." Dad nodded. "Just up the road. He was a year or two below your grandad at school."

"His name does ring a bell," Lennie said. "Was he in the first team?"

"He played for Liverpool in Europe," Dad said. "Somehow, it didn't quite happen for him after that. He had one great night –"

"When?" Lennie jumped in.

"It was the year I was born," Dad said. "1980. Liverpool were away to Bayern Munich. Gayle ran Bayern ragged."

"And he still didn't make it big at Liverpool?" Lennie said.

"No." Dad sighed. "Maybe it was racism, maybe it was bad luck, but it took Barnesy to change things. You know, some fans threw bananas on the pitch when a black player got the ball. When some idiot threw one at Barnesy, he just back-heeled it. Class." And he showed Lennie a photo of Barnesy doing just that.

But Lennie frowned – and not just at the old-school shorts. "Bad stuff happens in football. Why do we love it so much?"

"You know why," Dad said after a moment. "We can't let the idiots spoil it."

# BLACK PLAYERS IN BRITISH FOOTBALL

**Arthur Wharton**, from Ghana, was the world's first black professional footballer. He played in goal for Darlington and is commemorated with a statue at the FA's football centre in Burton.

**Walter Tull** was another black player in the early years of the game. He played for Spurs and Northampton Town. In 1909, away to Bristol City, Tull faced racist abuse. This is the first time racism in football is recorded. Tull was a hero of the First World War.

**Clyde Best**, born in Bermuda, was one of the first black players to play First Division football. He had to put up with racist chanting, but as a strong, powerful player who scored 47 goals for his team, he became a favourite at West Ham in the 1960s. He paved the way for other black footballers.

**Brendon Batson**, **Laurie Cunningham** and **Cyrille Regis** became famous at West Bromwich Albion in the 1970s as 'The Three Degrees'. They are hailed as helping other aspiring black players become professional footballers in the 1980s. In honour of Laurie Cunningham's impact on football, an English Heritage 'Blue Plaque' now marks the house where he grew up in London.

**Howard Gayle** was Liverpool F.C.'s first black player.  Gayle came from Liverpool 8, and he said, "I was proud to represent the black community of Liverpool."  He starred against Bayern Munich in the 1980–81 European Cup and played for lots of different clubs before he retired from football in 1993.

**John Barnes** is a Liverpool legend of the 1980s.  He had to deal with blatant racism during his career. With Liverpool he won the League championship twice, the FA Cup and the League Cup.  He was FWA Player of the Year twice and PFA Player of the Year once.  Barnes continues to speak out against racism in football – and in society as a whole.

# Chapter 5
# Nutmegged

Dad led the way down the garden path. Lennie hung back.

"Come on," Dad said. "United fans don't bite."

Grandad chuckled. "Well, not very often. You have to watch the vampire ones."

A man about Dad's age opened the front door. "Hey, Paul," he said as he gave Dad a hug.

"This is Marc," Dad said. "You know my dad, Viv."

Grandad shook Marc's hand, then Marc shook Lennie's hand too and led the way indoors. "Come and meet the twins."

Lennie followed the adults into the living room. The twins were waiting. And both of them were wearing Man U kits!

"This is Emma," Marc said, "and this is Katie."

Lennie stared. "You mean we're playing football with ... girls?"

Everybody laughed and they set off to the park where they put down hoodies for goals.

It was Liverpool v Man U. Emma was on the ball. Lennie went out to meet her, but she was past him in a flash. The ball went through his

legs and he fell on his bottom. Katie pulled him to his feet.

"She nutmegged me!" Lennie said.

"She'll do it again too," Marc said. "They're star players in our local league."

After the game, they went back to the house for something to eat. Marc and his wife Sophie brought in plates of sandwiches.

"What do you want to drink?" Sophie asked.

"Orange, please," Lennie said. "Hey, you're a Scouser."

"That's right," Sophie said with a grin. "We used to live in Liverpool. That's how Marc knows your dad. They were in the fire service together."

Dad nodded. "And that's why I don't like the nastiness between Liverpool and United," he said. "We were fighting a fire, about eight years ago, a big blaze. It was a nightmare, out of control. A whole wall came down."

"Like what happened to Grandad?" Lennie said.

"That's right," Dad said. "It could have been worse. I was trapped. Marc's the one who pulled the rubble off me and got me out. If it wasn't for him, I wouldn't be here to tell the tale."

Marc put his arm round Dad's shoulders.

"You would have done the same for me, mate," he said. "We're brothers."

Dad nodded. "Right, brothers. Always." He gave Lennie his long, hard look, the one he gave him when Lennie messed up. "So no more stupid chants, yeah?"

Lennie nodded and looked at Marc. "I did something stupid at the Europa match."

Marc nodded. "Your dad said."

Emma sat on the arm of her dad's chair. "Dad told a couple of guys to stop the Hillsborough chants."

Katie nodded. "We were all there. We got into a real row about it."

Now Lennie felt really stupid. "You must want to kick my backside."

Emma thought for a moment. "Only on the football pitch."

"We've got a new manager," Katie said. "We'll kick your backside next season."

Lennie pulled a face. "In your dreams," he said.

"That's what makes football special," Dad said with a grin. "Dreams. That's why it's our beautiful game."

Our books are tested
for children and young people by
children and young people.

Thanks to everyone who consulted on
a manuscript for their time and effort in
helping us to make our books better
for our readers.